ROB ROY

Nº 2

LIBRARY

1

THE OUTLAWED CHIEF

"For a moment Douglas quailed and shrank back, then, with
the valour of despair, he sprang towards Rob Roy with sword
uplifted."

THE OUTLAWED CHIEF

By ERSKINE BLAIR.

CHAPTER I.

A NEW WAY OF PAYING RENT.

"A SAD, savage country," said Peter Lambe, to himself, as he rode one evening through a Highland glen, and gazed moodily about him at the cloud-capped mountains.

"A sad, desolate land," he repeated; "but all lands are alike to one whose heart is desolate. Oh, Araminta!"

He breathed the name aloud, between a sigh and a groan, and his horse pricked its ears, believing itself to have been addressed by name, perhaps.

But Mr. Peter Lambe was apostrophising a fair but fickle damsel in distant London, and the horse, having decided that the name "Araminta" bore no resemblance to its usual appellation of "Jocky," drooped its head again, and crawled along the valley bottom at the pace most convenient to itself.

Peter Lambe was a well-favoured young man of five-and-twenty, passably rich, and newly come into the possession of a small estate near Callender, in Perthshire, which had been left to him by a Scottish kinsman, deceased.

Now, in the ordinary course of events, Peter would as soon have thought of taking up his residence in the Scottish Highlands as in Bedlam. Although born near the border, on the English side, he had lived long in London, and London, in the reign of Queen Anne, was a very

pleasant place to a young man of wit and fortune. The ordinary Londoner thought of Scotland much as a modern Londoner might think of the North Pole, or as a Parisian, accustomed to its leafy boulevards, thinks of any region outside the fortifications of Paris. But Araminta had proved false, so Peter welcomed the idea of living in exile, a broken-hearted hermit in his Scottish castle which, at present, he had never seen.

Scotsmen and their ways were still strange to him. He had seen much to marvel at in Edinburgh and Stirling, through both of which towns he had come; but it was not until he got among the mountains that he fully realised how far off he was from London and London ways.

He had sent his servant, Tom Tristram, on ahead, wishing to be alone with his own melancholy thoughts.

But in spite of his melancholy he began to feel hungry as the shades of night gathered about him; putting spurs to the indignant "Jocky," he pressed on, hoping to overtake his servant who had received some travelling directions at the last inn at which they had baited.

But instead of finding Tom Tristram, Peter rode into a thick mountain mist.

And now it was that he forgot Araminta, and thought longingly of peat fires and Scotch mutton.

"If I keep to the track, and 'tis a parlous rough one, I shall chance upon an inn in time," he told himself.

So he dismounted to make sure of not losing the track, and led his tired horse perseveringly forward.

The dark fell, and the mist was still cold on his face.

Araminta was quite forgotten now in the press of more immediate troubles. Mr. Peter Lambe was very hungry indeed, and cold and lonely besides.

"I would give a hundred guineas,"

he said, " to find myself yawning over the news-letter in a London coffee-house. 'Tis a pestilent country, this."

At last, when he was well-nigh reduced to despair, he saw a light through the mist.

He quickened his pace, to the annoyance of Jocky—who had but one pace, and that a very leisurely one—and presently found himself at the door of a stone-built farmhouse of very moderate proportions.

A tall man, wrapped in a plaid, stood before the door of the house.

" Good evening to you," said Peter.

" Good e'en to you, Southron," said the Scotsman, who spoke with a broad Scotch accent which we shall not attempt to reproduce.

" I hope," said Peter, " this is an inn for I have lost my way, and am starved, with cold."

" 'Tis no inn," said the other, " yet step inside. I may lack the shelter of a roof myself ere morning, I and mine, so I can feel compassion for homeless bodies. Are ye some pedlar ? "

Peter replied that peddling was not his calling, and, giving his horse to the Highlander, entered a warm, firelit room.

An old dame was nodding by the fire, and muttering to herself as she stared into the embers, and a girl was leaning over her with a beautiful look of solicitude in her blue eyes.

As Peter strode towards the fire, throwing back his cloak from his shoulders, the girl looked at him with quick alarm.

Peter, for his part, looked at her with wonder and admiration. Never anywhere, not even at the Court of St. James's, had he seen a more radiant creature than this gentle Highland girl.

In an instant he was bowing low. " Your servant, ladies," he said.

" Is it Killearn, or some poor lawyer body ? " asked the older woman, with asperity. " What ! he carries a sword ! Swords are for gentlemen to wear, sir, and not for them that war upon widows".

" You speak in riddles, madam," said Peter, " I trust the day may be far distant when I shall war upon widows, or any other women."

" Hech ! a poor Southron body ! " said the old woman, disdainfully. And then the man, having stabled Peter's horse, entered the room, and gave orders for supper to be set before the wayfarer.

" You are welcome to all we have," said the Highlander, " but it is little we shall have to give to any one after the morn."

The man's deep dejection, and the angry gloom of the old woman, told Peter that there was trouble in the house.

" Sir," he said to his host, " I see I have come upon you at a time of private misfortune, when a stranger's presence may be tedious."

" Nay, you are very welcome," replied the Highlander ; and Peter, rather mystified, sat down to a dish of mutton collops.

His hunger somewhat appeased, his curiosity began to increase ; and so, too, did his admiration for the beautiful Highland girl who had ministered to his wants.

While he had been supping Peter had been wondering how he should gain the confidence of his taciturn host. By the plaid he wore Peter, who had kept his eyes open during his stay in Edinburgh, knew him to be a MacGregor, and the MacGregors were Jacobites. Now Peter himself was a Tory and a Jacobite, and loyal to the King across the water, so, when he had a full noggin of whisky before him, he looked towards his host, and said, " I call a health MacGregor. Here's to King James."

The Highlander drank it and held out his hand.

" Give us your hand, man," he said, heartily, and Peter grasped it.

" Hech ! " said the old woman, " he's no so ill-favoured for a Southron, after all."

And then the Highlander's tongue was loosened, and he told Peter what his troubles were.

It seemed that it was rent day, but it had been a bad season, and MacGregor had not the wherewithal to pay what was due.

" Ay, it presses hardly upon us," said the Highlander, " but most heavily upon my mother, there, who has lived in this house all her life."

" A sorry case indeed," said Peter " Has your landlord no mercy ? "

" None," said the Highlander, " for I am a MacGregor, Killearn would give me time to pay what is due, but—I am MacGregor, and more, I have given shelter here to Rob Roy."

" Oho ! " said Peter, " I heard of him when I was in Edinburgh. He is highwayman, or some such thing, is he not?"

"Sir," said his host, "he is Chief of the Clan MacGregor."

"I ask your pardon," said Peter, humbly. "Then your landlord loves him not? Yet it is unjust to visit his sins upon you. Is your landlord a powerful man?"

"He is the Duke of Montrose, and Grahame of Killearn, who will be here anon, is his agent."

"And why does the Duke hate this man, Rob Roy?"

"Ah, 'tis an ill tale. The Duke of Montrose, you must know, and the Duke of Argyll are near neighbours, but Rob's land lies between theirs. Montrose would fain outcrow Argyll and have him disgraced, so he sought out Rob Roy and asked him to show that Argyll had had dealings with King James. 'If ye do this,' he said, 'I'll cancel your debts to me.' For Rob owed Montose money."

"So Rob Roy complied?"

"Man! Argyll is his friend. Would he betray his friend? He sent word of what Montrose was doing to Edinburgh, and the great Duke of Montrose was sore reproved. But he had his revenge upon Rob."

"Oh, he had?"

"Ay, he had him put to the horn."

"I am but a poor Southron," said Peter. "What might that signify?"

"It means that he had Rob outlawed for bankruptcy."

"So it is because you have sheltered an outlaw that you are to be turned out?"

"Ay, chiefly for that reason."

"But if the money were paid, Grahame could not vent his spite upon you thus?"

"No; he could not strain the law to suit his purpose so far."

"Does Rob Roy know of your plight?"

"I sent a message to him. I know not if it has reached him."

Peter was fingering some good Scotch bank-notes in his pocket, and furtively eyeing Mary MacGregor, who was gazing pensively into the fire.

He shuddered to think of her exposed to the raw air of the wintry night.

"MacGregor," he said, suddenly, "I came to your door as a beggar, but I am a rich man. I will pay your rent."

The Highlander's face flushed, and an angry light came into his eyes."

"Out upon Highland pride!" thought Peter. Then he said aloud, "I ask your pardon if I have put the matter too bluntly. I mean I will lend you the money to settle the Duke of Montrose's claim upon you."

"Sir," said the Highlander, "may you never be in want yourself. But, if you be, remember that the clan MacGregor are your friends, for this kindly deed shall not be hidden under a bushel."

While the Highlander was thanking Peter with great fervour, there was a knock at the door.

"'Tis the Duke's agent," said MacGregor.

"Pay him the uttermost farthing," said Peter, "and let him go."

The girl rose and unbarred the door blithely enough, giving Peter such a look of gratitude that he felt his loan was more than repaid already.

But instead of the Duke's agent a tall Highlander entered the room, a square-jawed man with reddish, curly hair, bushy eyebrows, and very keen eyes.

"Rob Roy!" cried Ian, springing to his feet, and grasping the hand of his chief, while Peter eyed the newcomer with great curiosity.

"You sent for me, Ian, and I have travelled night and day to reach you in time. You helped me when I was in need, and Rob Roy does not forget those who help him. You need money, Ian," said the chieftain.

"I need nothing now, Rob Roy. My guest, here, has lent me the money, and I can pay Grahame and send him about his business."

Rob Roy glanced at Peter and nodded. "Very good," he said, "be sure you get a full receipt, Ian."

"That will I. But you are not going, Rob Roy? You will sup with us, you and your men, for I think you have not come alone."

"I will go now and return later," replied Rob Roy, "for I think I hear horses on the track below. 'Tis Grahame come to claim what is due to him, and I would not meet him here, for fear it might harm you with the Duke. He will be a sorry man, Ian, when you discharge your debt." And with a laugh Rob Roy disappeared into the night again.

A minute later a cavalcade approached the door. The horsemen dismounted, and Grahame, of Killearn, with three followers, all booted and spurred, entered the room.

Old Mrs. MacGreggor drew herself up stiffly in her high-backed chair.

"What. Killearn, man," she said, "afraid to come into the country of the MacGregors without these poor gowks at your tail ?"

Killearn, disdaining to reply, turned to Ian MacGregor. "I have come about the business ye wot of," he said, "and no tale of an ill season will hinder me from doing my duty, MacGregor."

"We have no tales, ill or good, to spin ye," said Mrs. MacGregor, "unless you would hear how a great nobleman was put to shame for plotting the fall of his greater neighbour. Ay, that is an ill tale, sure enough."

Killearn, who was kin to the Duke of Montrose, frowned. One of his followers, whom he had chosen to supplant the Macgregors at their farm, was taking stock of the room.

"Mary," said Ian MacGregor, "set the ink-horn on the table and find Mr. Grahame, of Killearn, a clean pen."

As the girl obeyed, Killearn's face became gloomy, and the man who had supposed himself to be the incoming tenant looked woefully chap-fallen.

But Killearn had the money in his hand ; he was counting the notes, and could find no fault with them.

With an ill grace he sat down and wrote a receipt for the rent. His disappointed follower went after him to the door, and Peter drew his chair nearer to the blaze, well pleased to have been able to perform a kindly act.

And now he thought well to give the MacGregors some account of himself. He told them how, although an Englishman, he had recently become a Highland laird, and was journeying to see his property. But though he spoke much of London he said nothing of Araminta. To tell the truth, his mind's eye saw her face but vaguely now, for there was a fairer face for his eyes to dwell on, upon the opposite side of the hearth.

While Peter was yet talking with a degree of animation remarkable in a man who had recently resolved to be a hermit, the door opened once more, and in stepped Rob Roy.

The great chief approached Peter and held some banknotes out to him.

"Take back your money, sir," said Rob Roy, "and accept my thanks for the help you have rendered to my kinsman. If ever you are in trouble remember that the claymores of the MacGregors are at your service."

"Nay, sir," said Peter, "but may I not do your kinsman a service ? I am in no great haste for the discharge of the debt."

As he spoke he looked at the notes, they were the very ones that he had lent to MacGregor, and which he had seen MacGregor pay over to Killearn.

"How is this ?" he asked, in amazement.

Rob Roy laughed.

"There is no magic in it," he said, coolly. "I just took them back from Grahame. Have you the receipt, Ian ? 'Tis well. Oh, it is very well ! Killearn cannot trouble you till next rent day, for your debt to him and your debt to this gentleman are both discharged."

"You fought with them ?" asked Ian.

"Oh, it was nothing of a fight," said Rob Roy, carelessly. "I rifled his pockets and set him running. But can I lie here to-night, Ian, and my men will make shift with the straw in the stable ?"

Peter stared in astonishment at the great chief.

"A strange land," he told himself, "where country gentlemen practise highway robbery ! A strange land, indeed !" Peter heard much that was strange to him that night before he grew drowsy.

CHAPTER II.

Rob Roy's Bonnet.

The following morning Peter bade farewell to Ian MacGregor, and his mother and daughter, whom he hoped to see again, for his own house was not more than twenty miles distant from theirs.

And then, mounted once more upon "Jocky," he continued his journey, accompanied for some part of the way by Rob Roy and five of his clansmen, who were on foot.

He learnt that Rob Roy's house of Craigrostan had recently been seized by the Duke of Montrose, and that the Duke had, moreover, persuaded the Government to order the erection of a fort, which was even then in the course of building, at Inversnaid, upon Rob Roy's own land.

The fort was intended to overawe

the MacGregors, and to keep them in check.

While the Highland chief was telling Peter of these and other matters, they came upon a man who was seated by the wayside, disconsolately eyeing his horse, which latter was cropping the grass contentedly enough.

The man sprang up as they neared him, and Peter saw with satisfaction that it was his own servant, Tom Tristram. Tom was about thirty years of age. He was an honest, outspoken fellow, who had served in one of the Queen's regiments of Footguards, and who had accompanied his master to Scotland without protest, although he thought it a very poor sort of country indeed.

Seeing Mr. Lambe in company with half-a-dozen bare-legged Highlanders, he was at first rather non-plussed, believing him to have fallen among thieves. But when he considered that Mr. Lambe still retained his horse and sword, he felt reassured.

" Oh, sir," he said, " I am very glad to see you safe and sound, for I have had some anxiety upon your account."

" I am well enough, Tom," said Peter. " Did you think I had gone astray in the mist ? "

" No, sir, but I thought, perhaps, you had been waylaid, for now I know this is a very perilous country. I am glad you have got an escort." But for all that he looked rather askance at Rob Roy and his men, who had come to a halt beside Peter.

" And how have you fared, Tom ? " asked Peter.

" Why, sir, I have not fared so badly, for I found an inn which stands further up the road, so I had a dry bed."

" And a warm supper, I trust ? "

Tom made a wry face. " As to that, sir, the people of the inn fed me with oats which is only fit for horses, and I do not like the wine of the country, though it warms the blood, and may stave off the agues bred by the fog."

" Well, well, I trust you slept well, Tom," continued his master.

" Nay, sir, for when I was beginning to nod there came in a man who squeezed music out of a bag, which music, sir, was nothing comparable to the music of drums and fifes, but resembled rather the squealing of a pig. And when he was done there came in some very honest

gentlemen who had been robbed on the road by a notable highwayman who infests these parts, a rascal who goes by the name of Rob Roy."

Peter was about to reprove his servant, but Rob Roy, with a smile, put a finger upon his lips, so Peter allowed Tom to run on.

" It seems, sir, that this Rob Roy steals the cattle of the gentlemen and noblemen hereabouts, and none can lay hands upon him. He has been turned out of his house, which makes him the more deseperate. But there is one thing which is in his favour, your honour, for they say that he stands well with the King across the water. But for all that I feared you might have fallen into his hands and been robbed."

" Nay," said Peter, smiling ; " if you were turned out of your house by a great nobleman would you not consider yourself entitled to attack that nobleman's servants ? "

" That I should, sir," replied Tom. " I would lose no opportunity of trouncing them."

" Well, the gentleman whom you saw last night were servants of the Duke of Montrose, who has used Rob Roy very ill. And this is Rob Roy himself, the chief of a great clan."

Tom doffed his hat to the chief. " Indeed, I ask your pardon, sir," he said. " I trust your honour will think no worse of me for what I have said. I am, all unused to this country, and you must know that in England gentlemen do not make free with one another's cattle ; but I see it is here the custom of the country, and I wish your honour good luck in driving of your neighbours' herds."

Rob Roy laughingly thanked Tom Tristram, and then once more very earnestly assured Peter that he and his clan would aid him if ever he got into any trouble with his Whiggish neighbours ; for party feeling ran very high at that time, and if it became known that Peter was a Jacobite he might find himself in difficulties with the Government.

After that they travelled on again. They passed the inn where Tom had spent the night, and where Killearn and his men had also found shelter, and Peter was about to part company with Rob Roy, when from among th rocks bordering the road, a dozen sturd ellows suddenly sprang up, all armed with claymores.

In an instant Rob Roy drew his sword, and ran forward to meet these fierce swordsmen, whom he recognised as partizans of the Duke of Montrose. Killearn was not amongst them, but he guessed that this ambush had been planned by Killearn.

Rob Roy's clansmen, taken by surprise, did not immediately follow their chief, who was guarding himself against the attack of three swordsmen at once.

Fearing his new friend would be struck down, Peter spurred his horse, drew his sword, and dashed forward to his rescue.

He saw, with dismay, a claymore descend upon Rob Roy's head, cleave his bonnet, and fell him to the ground. The next instant he was fighting fiercely with the man who had brought down the chief; and then the MacGregors, with Tom Tristram in their midst, charged past him with wild yells, and the Duke's men scattered swiftly amongst the rocks.

The tussle over, Peter, with genuine sorrow, turned, expecting to see Rob Roy's lifeless body. To his surpirse he saw, instead, that the red-haired chief was upon his feet, apparently none the worse for the terrific blow that had been dealt at his pate.

"Man," said Rob Roy, coming forward, "you're a bonny fighter, and I am more than ever your debtor. The MacGregors will not forget this day, and neither, by the same token, will the Grahames."

"By what charm was your life spared?" said Peter, in astonishment. "The rascal dealt a shrewd blow at your head, and your bonnet is cut in two, and you none the worse for it!"

"Ay! I dented the Grahame body's claymore," said Rob Roy, gravely. "'Twas no magic, Mr. Lambe, but a wee plate of iron that I wear in my bonnet to guard against mischances."

Tom, who had been staring open-mouthed at the chief, wondering what his head could be made of, now burst into laughter.

"Rob Roy for ever!" he cried; "and I see we have come to a fine country for diversion. Give us your hand, man."

As they continued upon their way,

Peter privately reproved his servant for this familiarity.

"You must know," he said, "that this Rob Roy is a great landowner and a gentleman, whose father was a colonel in the service of King Charles, and you must not treat him as if he was your equal, you rascal!"

"I ask your pardon, sir, and his," said Tom; "but it is parlous strange to me to see a gentleman going without knee-breeches, and dressed like a wild man in a booth at Bartholomew Fair. But I shall get used to the ways of this country in time, though I hope your honour will not have me to eat oats, as the fashion is here, for it is flying in the face of Nature, oats being, as all men know, only suitable for horses and asses. And now, sir, I think these bare-legged gentlemen are waiting to bid us good-day."

The MacGregors, who had been marching in advance of Peter and his servant, had certainly come to a halt, and Rob Roy explained to Peter that they must part at this point.

"Yonder is your house, Garoch," he said, calling Peter, as is the custom in Scotland, by the name of his estate. "And if ever you want help send word to a MacGregor. The late laird was a Whig, and we often drove his kye, but the new laird's cattle shall be safe, and that without payment of any blackmail."

Peter thanked the chief with becoming gratitude, and, after a ceremonious leave-taking, went forward towards his house, while the bare-legged clansmen scrambled up a hillside after their chief, and disappeared among the gloomy crags.

CHAPTER III.

THE FORT OF INVERSNAID.

"You must know, sir, that they manage things very differently here from what they do in England."

Tom Tristram was talking to his master upon the morning after their arrival at their new home.

"Indeed, Tom," said Peter, "and how so?"

"Why, sir, in these parts a gentleman's tenants and servants all bear the same name as himself, and claim to be his kinsmen, and the gentleman is called a chief, and the people are called his clan. Every clan is at war with every other clan, and the clansmen obey their chiefs without regard to the law of the land. And the chief comes before the king or queen, which is a bad thing for the country."

" Pray where did you acquire all this learning ? " said Peter, smiling.

" I was talking to the young man who is the son of your housekeeper, sir, and who, it seems, keeps your garden in order. He had a great respect for the late laird, your honour, for they were of the same clan, but he has none at all for you, as you are not of any clan. And he says that if you had not won Rob Roy's favour the Highlanders would have stolen your cattle and burnt your house, for they cannot endure people from the Lowlands."

" A pleasant country, truly," said Peter. " So none respect the law in these parts ? "

" No, sir, save only the great nobles who go to Court to seek royal favour, and they will keep their tenants in some order. But the wilder sort of chiefs are like kings in their own country, and all the Highland men think it a great disgrace to do any work. "

" Very well," said Peter, " but since we are not Highlanders we will think otherwise. Go now, and saddle my horse."

For some weeks Peter lived quietly enough, a stranger in a strange land, speaking to few people save his servants, and quietly observing what went on about him. He heard many tales of lawless deeds, but so far his own property was secure from violence. That he was regarded by his own servants as an interloper, he knew ; and he would very speedily have retired from the kingdom of Scotland altogether but for two reasons ; firstly, he loved Mary MacGregor, whom he contrived to see from time to time ; and, in the second place, a Jacobite rising was probable in Scotland, and Peter wished to have a hand in any attempt that was made to restore the rightful king, as he considered him, to the throne.

So Mr. Peter Lambe, cured of his heart-sickness, dwelt in his house among the mountains, until, one winter's morning he saw a band of men, wearing the Campbell tartan, approaching his door.

The chief person among these Campbells was a dour looking fellow who rode on horseback, his followers being on foot.

Suspecting no harm, Peter's servants admitted this Campbell, who no sooner saw Peter than he asked him by what right he held the house of Garoch.

" By what right ? " asked Peter, angrily. " By the right of inheritance, to be sure ; and I would like to know, since you talk of rights, by what right you come here to question me."

" I shall show you my right soon enough," said Campbell. " You say you got your house by inheritance. But by what right did he who left you the land hold it ? Have ye the title deeds ? "

Peter knew of no deeds, or documents, but he was not going to argue the matter with any one.

" I don't know who you are," he said to his unwelcome visitor, " but you are a mighty impertinent fellow."

" And I know you," said Campbell, " for a Jacobite, and a friend of that noted chief and outlaw, Rob Roy, and so I have come here armed with a legal warrant to evict you from this house, which, in default of any one showing better title to it, is the property of the Crown."

Peter and his visitor were alone while this conversation was taking place, but now Peter rang a bell to summon Tom Tristram.

" It is my intention," he said, hotly, " to order my servant to evict you from this room ; and if you ask for my warrant to turn you out you will find it here," and he tapped his sword hilt. At that, Campbell stamped his foot upon the floor ; the door of the room burst open, and a dozen armed Campbells crowded tumultuously in. Tom Tristram, his face red with wrath, brought up the rear.

" Wait till you're asked to enter a gentleman's room, can't you, you bare-legged knaves ? " he said, striving to push the sturdy clansmen out of the door. " I would some of you were in my old regiment, and I were your sergeant, you red whiskered rascals ; I would teach you respect for your betters. Go home to your oat - mash, you lubbers."

But the Highlanders preferred to take their orders from their chieftain, and it was plain to Peter that he was to be excluded from his own house by force. Perhaps this show of force was sanctioned by the laws of Scotland, but the English laird was not the man to submit tamely to such treatment.

He allowed himself, indeed, to be ushered out of the room; but then, calling to Tom to follow him, he ran across the hall into another chamber, and shut a heavy oak door in the faces of the Campbells.

"Are these morning visits a fashion of the country, sir?" said Tom.

"This fellow, who is kinsman to the great Duke of Argyll, claims to have a right to turn me out of my house," said Peter, breathing quick with anger. "He may have law on his side, since, it seems, I am a known Jacobite, but——"

"But," said Tom, squaring his shoulders and waving his fists towards the door, "but we will make a fight for it."

"The thing has happened so suddenly, or I would have made preparations to greet this fellow," continued Peter. "Can we get at any arms? I have my sword."

"Alas! I have only my two hands," said Tom. At that moment the door was forced open, and the Highlanders crowded in, their chieftain taking good care to keep well in the rear.

Tom Tristram had the satisfaction of planting his fist in the eye of the foremost clansman, but, after delivering that one doughty blow, he was seized by three or four men. He still struggled, however, and brought his opponents to the ground, where he continued to kick and wrestle, until exhausted.

Peter, meanwhile, with his drawn sword, retreated to a corner of the room, and invited the chieftain to meet him in single combat.

But two or three men with claymores beat at his sword till it was struck from his hand, so he, too, was overpowered.

After that he and Tom Tristram were, without ceremony, hustled out of the house.

There was no law to appeal to in that lawless country. It would be worse than vain to appeal to Argyll, who would probably approve of his kinsman's act. Peter might, of course, travel to Edinburgh, where there were courts of law. But Edinburgh was far away, and the Campbells in favour with the ruling Powers.

And so Mr. Peter Lambe found himself homeless, upon a bitter winter's morning.

"If I may advise you, sir," said Tom

"I should go at once to that gentleman who wears the iron plate in his hat—to Sir Rob Roy, or whatever his name and title may be. He is a much better man than this poor rascal who has done us this ill-turn, and he promised you help if ever you got into trouble with your neighbours."

"I believe you are right, Tom," said Peter; "he is an outlaw, and if I go to him I shall, perhaps, be outlawed myself; but I will certainly be revenged upon this man Campbell, and I think Rob Roy will be glad to be of service to me."

He and Tom Tristram managed to secure two horses before the Campbells began to investigate the stables, and, quickly mounting, they rode off to the house of Ian MacGregor, which they reached before nightfall.

Peter poured out the tale of his woes to Ian.

"Ay," said the latter at the conclusion of it, "I ken this Campbell. He's kinsman to Argyll, and a noted plotter against Jacobites, and against all small land-owners who cannot produce documentary proof that the lands they hold are their own. He is a dangerous man, for it is by favour of the Government that he turns poor men out of their homes. So he did to a MacGregor not long since, and so he tried to do to a Maclean. But Maclean was ready for him, for he had hidden his men all about his house, and when this Campbell body asked Maclean by what charter he held his lands, up rose his clansmen with their claymores, all round him. 'These,' said Maclean, 'are the charters by which I hold my lands, as my forefathers did before me.'"

"But I have no clansmen," said Peter, "and my tenants love me not. 'Tis enough to drive a man into open rebellion to be treated thus by the friends of the Government. I shall go to seek your chief, Rob Roy. Know you where I shall find him?"

Rob Roy, it appeared, was lurking near his own house of Craigrostan, from which, as we have said, he had been evicted by the Duke of Montrose as an outlaw.

So the homeless English laird set out with his servant in search of the homeless Scottish chief.

"For my own part, sir," said Tom, as they rode among the mountains towards Craigrostan, "I should not, were I in your shoes, regard the loss of the house at Garoch as of much consequence. Your honour is rich, and only came into this country, if I may say so, because of a fit of the spleen; and the house at Garoch is an ill, draughty place, where there is no amusement either for a gentleman or his man. No; were I in your shoes, I should ride and never stop until I was across the Border, in England, which I take to be the only country fit for a gentleman to live in."

"Silence!" said Peter. "I shall do no such thing. 'Tis not that I care about this house; but I will certainly have my revenge upon this man Campbell, who is no better than a thief."

"I grant you that," said Tom, who was not to be silenced, "and if you can set a bigger thief on to him, we shall certainly see some sport. Very well, sir; I had half a mind to discharge myself from your service, but now I will stay and see the fun."

"I should be sorry to lose you, Tristram; yet, perhaps, I am not doing right to lead you into dangers," said Peter. "Cross the Border, by all means, if you think it to your interest to do so."

"No, sir," said Tom, "I will stand by you, and you must not call me Tristram, either, for now my name is Lambe."

"How? You are impertinent," said Peter.

"No, sir, I do not mean to be. But it does not become one of your dignity to be without a clan, to steal for you and follow you to the wars. And since I am all the clan you have I must needs take your name. 'Tis the fashion of the country, sir."

"You are a ridiculous fellow," said Peter. "But here is a man that wears the MacGregor tartan. He may have tidings of Rob Roy."

The MacGregor, who was one of those who had been with Rob Roy in the recent skirmish with the Grahames, recognised Peter, and readily agreed to conduct him to the hiding-place of his chief.

The snow was falling when Peter arrived at the lonely house where Rob Roy was, at present, dwelling. The great chief received him very cordially and listened to the tale of his wrongs.

"I shall have somewhat to say to Campbell," he said, at last, "but to-night I have work of my own to do." And his keen eyes twinkled.

"I trust," said Peter, "you will let me help you."

"'Twill bring you into no favour with the Government."

"A fig for the Government," retorted Peter; "and since I have found no friends in Scotland, save among the MacGregors, I am ready to throw in my lot with the MacGregors."

"And so am I," said Tom Tristram, who was sampling the MacGregor's whiskey in company with several sturdy members of the clan, for the room was full of kilted clansmen.

Peter's sentiment was warmly applauded, and he was presently informed that the MacGregors were, that very night, going to take the Fort of Inversnaid, which had just been built by the Government in the heart of the MacGregor country, to keep the wild MacGregors in order.

Now Tom Tristram had served in the Low Countries and had seen many fortified places taken.

"But, sir," he said to his master, "I do not see how a few half-naked men, armed only with claymores, are going to take a fort. There must be artillery, and trenches, and a regular siege, before a fortress can be taken. And it must either be reduced by famine, or else carried by assault, when the walls have been breached—and we have no cannon. I fear that this Rob Roy is not a very skilled soldier, or he would know all this as well as I do. But to be sure, they call your house a castle when it is no castle at all, so perhaps this fort of Inversnaid is no fort, according to the meaning of the word in England."

"We shall see in good time," said Peter, while the wind howled outside the house and the Highlanders made merry over their whisky, and over their forthcoming adventure.

The ground was white with newly fallen snow when Rob Roy and his little band set out towards the fort of Inversnaid.

Wrapped in their plaids the sturdy clansmen tramped on through the snow and the darkness, until at length the fort loomed before them.

It was, as Tom Tristram had to admit, a formidable place. Situated upon the top of a hill, it consisted of two high buildings, enclosed within a tall outer wall, which was surmounted by battlements, and the ex-guardsman of Marlborough's wars wondered exceedingly how Rob Roy proposed to take possession of it.

But the chief led his men boldly up the hill, until they were brought to a standstill by the outer wall of the fort. Ranging his men under the wall he went up to the outer gate of the fort and knocked upon it loudly.

Presently a voice was heard on the other side of the gate.

" Who's there ? "

" A poor traveller," whined Rob Roy. " Let me in, or I shall perish in the snow."

The howl of the wintry wind accompanied his petition. There was some talk audible on the other side of the gate, and then the compassionate gate-keeper unbarred the heavy portal. In a moment, as if blown in by the wind, the kilted MacGregors, with their claymores drawn, dashed through the gate, and the slogan or war-cry of the clan rose above the shrieks of the tempest.

Rob Roy caught hold of an astonished gentleman within the walls, who chanced to be the builder, and threatened instant death to everyone in the fort if his clansmen were resisted.

Now the fort was only just completed, and its only occupants were the builder and his workmen. Seeing that resistance was useless the builder, whose name was Nasmyth, together with his workmen, yielded themselves prisoners.

The MacGregors speedily bound the unfortunate workmen, and then warmed themselves by the fire, round which the workmen had been making merry.

" I see now," said Tom Tristram to his master, as they stood by the fire, " that Sir Rob Roy is a very skilful officer, and I will own that a nimble brain may be of more service than cannon-balls. But what is he going to do with the prisoners ? "

Rob Roy himself answered this question by ordering half his company of clansmen to remain to garrison the fort, while the other half accompanied him.

" I will send Montrose's workmen back to him," he said, " and thank him for having built me a stout fort."

The prisoners were, accordingly, marched out of the fort, through the snow, towards Craigrostan, which was full of Montrose's men.

At a little distance from the house the prisoners were unbound.

" You shall swear," said Rob Roy to them, " you will never more return to the country of the MacGregors."

The dejected builder swore, and then, with his workmen, vanished towards Craigrostan, while the chief of the MacGregors returned to the fort, which had been built to keep him in subjection, but which was to serve him as a place of refuge from which he could defy his powerful enemy.

CHAPTER IV.

A CATTLE RAID.

" If your honour is for an airing," said Tom Tristram one morning to Peter, " you may go out and steal cows."

The tall guardsman was brushing Peter's clothes, while Peter himself was yet incumbent in bed. An apartment which had been designed, probably, for officers' quarters had been allotted to Mr. Lambe in the fort, for he intended to remain with Roy Roy until the latter should be able to retake the house of Garoch.

" Steal cows ? " ejaculated Peter, sleepily. " What should I want with cows ? "

" 'Tis a custom of the country," said Tom, " to steal your neighbour's cows, just as it is your honour's custom, when in England, to hunt the deer or the fox."

" Ay, to be sure," said Peter, now fully awake; " is the chief going out to lift cattle ? "

" The MacGregor clan," replied Tom, ' is going out to steal the Duke's cattle, and I think, if I may say so, that the Lambe clan should not be backward in the business."

" Had you told me six months ago that I should ever steal other men's cattle, Tom, I should have called you a madman," remarked Peter.

" Yes, sir," said Tom, " 'tis strange sport for a gentleman, and in England would bring one to the gallows. I have stolen many a fat hen when I was campaigning in Flanders, but never yet stole a cow, and I should like to see the sport."

" Very well," said Peter," we will go out with the MacGregors. And now I will dress."

While Mr. Lambe was clothing himself, and wondering what his friends at the

London coffee houses would say of his new occupations, he heard a sound in an adjoining compartment as of a creature in agony. Squeals and groans, mingled with a man's angry ejaculations, The walls were thick, and Peter could not at first decide upon the exact nature of the sounds.

Hastily finishing his toilet he went into the room whence the sound came. There he saw Tom wrestling with a bag-pipe, his face red and distended, striving to extract music from the instrument, while a Highlander looked on gravely throwing in words of instruction and advice.

"I can play upon the whistle-pipe," said Tom, "but get music out of this bag I cannot. Nay, I will give it one more squeeze."

The result of his exertions was a ghastly squeal, which moved Peter to laughter.

Tom looked up at that.

"I fear I shall have to give it up, sir," he said.

"I think you will, Tom," said his master; "I did not know you aspired to be a piper."

"'Tis this way you see, sir. Every chief in this country has his piper, and I thought that for the support of your dignity, you being laird of Garoch, and chief of the Lambe clan, you should have one also."

"Thank you," said Peter, "but I scarcely think it would add to my dignity to have you going before me and making such discordant noise. I must be content to do without some of the honours of chieftainship. For example, I have no tartan, no kilt."

"Oh! no, sir," said Tom, hastily; "if you are thinking of dressing your clan in kilts I shall go back across the Border. 'Tis no Christian fashion, surely, that men should wear petticoats, and in this cold weather, too!"

"Have no fear," laughed Peter; "I have no wish to dress you in any such livery. But we must be stirring."

A few minutes later Rob Roy was ready to sally forth, and Tom was provided with a firelock, with the use of which he was better acquainted than he was with the use of bagpipes. Rob Roy himself carried a pistol, and a claymore or broadsword, and his clansmen all wore claymores and dirks.

The ground was now clear of snow, and after an arduous march the little band entered a glen where a herd of cattle was grazing, tended by two or three armed herdsmen, for at that time the Highlanders wore their arms even when engaged in the most peaceful occupations.

At the head of the glen the tower of a castle showed above the rocks.

Rob Roy ordered his men to advance up the glen through a plantation, so as to avoid attracting the attention of the herdsmen, and then to interpose themselves between the castle and the herd.

After a hurried, noiseless march, the MacGregors accompanied, as Tom Tristram said in telling of the raid, by the Lambes, ran out into the middle of the valley, and, shouting their slogan, charged down upon the herd, Tom shouting a war cry of his own.

The startled herdsmen were unable to get to the castle to give the alarm, and when they saw that their foes were the dreaded MacGregors, they lost no time in scrambling up the hillside and disappearing, while Rob Roy's men drove off the cattle at their leisure.

Committing the beasts to the care of his men, Rob Roy then set off, accompanied only by Peter, to visit a tenant of the Duke of Montrose's who lived hard by.

Peter expressed some surprise that the chief should visit his enemy's tenants.

"You must know," said Rob Roy, "that I collect his Grace's rents."

At which Peter wondered more than ever.

After a long walk they came to an isolated farm, and Rob Roy, without ceremony, entered the house, with his broadsword drawn.

It was a large comfortable house, and the farmer, a Grahame, was a comfortable looking man.

But his consternation was great when he saw Rob Roy.

Hand over your siller, farmer," said Rob Roy; "I have come to collect your rent."

"'Tis only to Killearn or the Duke himself that I'll pay my rent," said the farmer.

"Come! Needs must when the de'il drives," replied Rob Roy. "Montrose has taken my land, and I'll take his gold."

Grumblingly the farmer retired to another room, and returned with a purse of gold. He counted out the amount of his rent, and Rob Roy gave him a receipt for it " on account of Montrose."

And now the farmer's manner seemed to change, and he pressed his visitors to sit down and take a glass of whisky.

Lest he should seem to be afraid to dally in the midst of the Grahame's country, Rob Roy accepted the invitation, and he and Peter were regaled with food and drink.

They had been about half-an-hour in the house when Rob Roy finally rose to depart.

As he did so he chanced to glance out of the window, and his brow contracted with wrath.

" Ay, you have put a fine trick upon me, Grahame," he said, " you have sent word to your kinsmen that I was here while we drank your whisky."

But the farmer had vanished from the room, and there were six men in the Grahame tartan approaching the house.

Peter now drew his sword, and gave himself up for lost, for he felt certain that he would very shortly have to appear at Montrose's castle in the unpleasant rôle of a prisoner and a cattle-thief. The Grahames were all strong, determined men, and the odds were six to two.

But Rob Roy stood by the door sword in hand, smiling grimly.

They heard the farmer call out from one of the windows of the house that Rob Roy was within, and then the door was kicked open and a fierce bearded fellow strove to enter.

Instantly Rob Roy's sword crossed his. The chief was fighting for his life in real earnest, for he was an outlaw, and any man who killed him would be legally justified.

The doorway was too narrow to admit of two men standing in it, so Peter had to remain a spectator of the fight.

He soon regained confidence when he saw Rob Roy's skill with the claymore, and his extraordinary length of arm.

The foremost of the attacking party reeled back, severely wounded, and his place was taken by another fiercer than himself. Rob Roy's sweeping blade descended on the second man's bonnet like a flash of lightning, and he, too, fell.

The enraged Grahames strove now to enter the doorway two abreast, and at the same moment the farmer came into the room with a loaded gun, thinking to shoot Rob Roy from behind. But the English laird rushed at him so furiously that he retired without discharging his weapon, and when Peter looked round at the open doorway again he saw four men prostrate before the threshold, while Rob Roy was taunting the two remaining Grahames, who had retired some little way from the house, with cowardice.

" Follow me, Garoch," said Rob Roy.

Peter stepped over the fallen men, and followed the chief, who walked disdainfully past the two men who had not come within reach of his sword, and who now showed no intention of doing so, but went to the assistance of their wounded companions.

Rob Roy then led Peter by a circuitous way back towards the fort where he had already been sheltered for some days.

The young Englishman was by no means satisfied with his present position, although hospitably treated. He was anxious to eject the intruders from his own house, and was beginning, at the time of the raid into Montrose's country, to grow impatient for the assistance Rob Roy had promised him.

He was relieved, therefore, when the chief said to him, as they were nearing the fort, " We've had a bonny fight to-day with the proud Grahames ; to-morrow it will be the crafty Campbells that shall hear our slogan at your house of Garoch, Mr. Lambe. I am, I hope, a leal friend to the Duke of Argyll, and my own mother was a Campbell, but this thieving knight that turns honest men out of their houses shall not shelter under the wing of Argyll, kin to him though he be."

" I thank you for your promised help," said Peter ; " but who is this that follows us to the fort ? " For a man was hastening after them through the growing dusk.

" I think it is Ian MacGregor," said Rob Roy, turning. " Ay, and there is surely some trouble come upon him that he hastens to me so fast. How now, Ian ? " he cried aloud, as the grey-haired Highlander drew near to them, " is there aught amiss at your house ? "

Ian MacGregor, although a hardy man, was almost dropping with fatigue by the time he came up to his two friends, and it was evident that he had been travelling at a great pace. So breathless was he that he could not at first explain his mission.

" Have Montrose's men been troubling you again ? " said Rob Roy, sternly.

" If they have carried off your cattle I will make your loss good out of Montrose's own herd."

" They have not touched my cattle," panted Ian, " and you cannot make good my loss. There came four men when I was away from home this morning, and they have carried away my daughter, to make her Jamie Douglas's wife."

Peter uttered a cry of dismay and anger, and he turned expectantly towards Rob Roy, thinking he would be as enraged as himself at the news of this outrage. To his surprise Rob Roy was smiling.

" Ay, ay, Ian," he said, " it is no new fashion among us, surely, that a bridegroom should carry off his bride, and Jamie Douglas, though I know him not, is well able to dress his wife in silk and——"

" Is it silk dresses she will be wanting?" said Ian scornfully. " The lassie would sooner wear a winding-sheet than be Jamie Douglas's bride. And my mother, who is a wise woman, told me that this affair was planned by the Grahames, for Duncan Grahame was with Douglas when they carried off my daughter."

Rob Roy's brow grew darker at mention of Duncan Grahame, who had incurred his enmity in some way, and he said that he was ready at once to send men to attempt the rescue of Mary MacGregor.

" I will be one of them," said Peter, turning to Ian ; " we must not delay a moment."

" You forget, Garoch, we have work to do in the Campbell country," said Rob Roy.

" Oh ! that can wait. What is my house compared with Mary MacGregor ? I would sooner see it given to the flames than learn that one hair of her head had been harmed. Come, sir, to the fort, to muster the men ! There is not a moment to lose."

" Ay ! " said Rob Roy, " no lass of the MacGregor clan shall be married against her will, and if your daughter is in truth unwilling, Ian, the claymores of the MacGregors shall all be red before any harm befalls her."

With that they hurried up the hill and into the fort, where a score of MacGregors were exulting over their successful raid into Montrose's territory.

CHAPTER V.

A WEDDING.

The snow was falling when the rescue party left the fort of Inversnaid, and set off in the direction of the wild country in the neighbourhood of Loch Lomond.

Peter had been afoot almost all day, but he was too anxious to feel any fatigue, as he led the way with Mary's father.

" It will be a wild night, Mr. Lambe," said the latter, " and you have been out all day. I am grateful for your help, but I should counsel you to bide at home."

" Nay, I claim the right to be at your side to-night, MacGregor," said Peter, his face pale with emotion.

" The right, Garoch ? " said Ian MacGregor, surprised at something in the English laird's tones.

" Yes," replied Peter, " for I love your daughter. I am a landless man this side of the border, unless Rob Roy can vindicate my rights, but I have possessions south of the border, and if your daughter will marry me I will take her there, MacGregor, for I do not wish to live always amidst strife and bloodshed. Yet, to-night, you may be sure, after what I have told you, that I shall be foremost in any fighting there may be with Douglas's men."

" Give me your hand, Garoch," said Ian. " I think the lassie likes you well."

" Can she be married against her will ? " asked Peter, who was a prey to the most painful anxieties.

" Such weddings do take place in Scotland," replied Ian, " and, indeed, it is thought right in most cases for a maiden to feign reluctance. But there is no feigning here. Douglas is a dour, ill-favoured man, and over friendly with the Grahames. He has always been civil to me, but now I see the meaning of his civility."

" Are we going to his house ? "

" Yes, but first of all to the house of his sister, where it is thought he would carry Mary, for it lies on his homeward road, and has, besides, a private chapel, where a wedding could be celebrated after the forms of the Catholic faith, for Douglas and his kindred are Roman Catholics."

" And would any priest be base enough to marry a reluctant bride ? "

" Yes, under compulsion."

Peter marched on more swiftly, the

soft snowflakes blowing in his face. Behind him followed Rob Roy with six of his clansmen, all armed with claymores, and Tom Tristram who shouldered a firelock.

As snow was falling heavily, all traces of Douglas's progress amidst the lonely mountains were obliterated; but Ian MacGregor knew the way to the castle near the shores of Loch Lomond, where dwelt Douglas's sister who had married a Grahame.

It was about midnight when the rescue party reached the gate of the castle. There was a light burning in the chapel, and the pointed windows of this building, with their delicate stone tracery, stood out clearly in the darkness.

"The wedding is even now in progress," said Peter, "but it cannot, it shall not be accounted a legal wedding, even if the ceremony is already over."

"Have no fear, Garoch," said Rob Roy, "the sword shall dissolve it. If Mary be wedded to Douglas, she shall be widowed before they go in to the wedding feast. I think the ceremony is not yet over. Knock at the door, Garoch, and ask admission. They will not suspect an English voice."

The English laird, accordingly, drew near to the main door of the castle and knocked loudly upon it. At last a manservant opened a little hatch in the upper part of the ponderous door and looked out.

"Who is that knocking?" he asked.

"I am an English traveller and have lost my way in the snow," said Peter. "For heaven's sake let me in, or I shall be frozen to death."

A Scotsman, either from the Highlands or Lowlands, might have failed to gain admission to the castle, but the gatekeeper had no reason for suspecting an Englishman and slowly unfastened the door.

The next moment he repented heartily of his compassionate behaviour, for Rob Roy had him by the throat behind the door.

"See to it," said the chief, to one of his clansmen, "that this rogue gives no alarm."

Then he passed on into the house, with his followers at his heels.

Another servant was surprised in the castle hall and forced into silence.

"Lead us to the chapel," said Rob Roy to the terrified man, holding a dirk to his throat as he spoke.

The servant led them softly to a curtained doorway. Peter and Rob Roy alone slipped through the curtains, leaving the rest of the party to come to their aid if summoned.

It was a strange and striking scene which met Peter's gaze. At the end of the jewelled, dimly lighted chapel stood the priest, facing the door. On each side of him was a man armed with a dirk.

In front of the priest stood Jamie Douglas, a swart, fierce-looking fellow, and opposite Douglas was Mary Mac-Gregor, supported by a harsh-featured elderly woman. The bridal party was hedged round with steel, for nine or ten men with claymores drawn were gathered about the altar. It was plain that the priest and the bride were both unwilling participants in the ceremony.

From the hum of voices at the end of the chapel certain words seemed to detach themselves.

"Look up at your husband, pretty fool," Peter heard a feminine voice exclaim. "Your tears and your sighs are of no avail. The priest has made you his wife ——"

"Compelled by threats to do so," put in the priest, in a clear, resonant voice that was unmistakably Irish.

"No matter for that," continued the elder woman; "I say she is Jamie's wife, and not all the lawyers of Scotland can undo the knot that you have tied."

Rob Roy, hidden in the dark folds of the curtains, said in a hollow voice, "Steel is stronger than parchment."

"Who spoke?" asked the mistress of the castle, and all looked down the chapel towards the door.

"'Tis one of the servants," said Douglas.

"You lie, Douglas," continued Rob Roy, in the same hollow tones as before.

There was a hushed silence near the altar, and a look of awe upon all faces. It was a superstitious age, and the Scots were a superstitious race. Who was this unbidden guest with the spectral voice who dared to flout the bridegroom?

Douglas resolved to answer this question for himself. With drawn sword he came down the aisle of the vaulted chapel. The unhappy bride was by now insensible, and had not noticed the intruder's voice. As Douglas neared the door, Rob Roy stepped out from the folds of the curtains, claymore in hand.

There was no man whom the bride-groom less wished to see than the chief of the clan from which he had stolen his bride, for he knew Rob Roy's anger would be great.

For a moment he quailed and shrank back. Then, with the valour of despair, he sprang towards Rob Roy with sword uplifted. The chief caught the blow that followed upon his claymore, and the noisy clash of steel filled the building.

Without awaiting their leader's orders the MacGregors rushed into the chapel. Peter saw swords glimmer and flash in the lamplight; and James Douglas was lying prone upon the stone flags of the chapel aisle, cut down by half-a-dozen blades at once.

The bride was a widow, and she alone knew it not, for she was still insensible.

Meanwhile, the friends of Douglas had advanced half-way down the chapel. Upon that the MacGregors raised their fierce slogan, and a terrific fight must have ensued, but for the fact that at that moment some one put out the altar lights, and the place was in darkness. No man dared to strike a blow, for fear of injuring his friends in the darkness.

The chapel was filled with wild cries, above which Peter heard Rob Roy's voice. The chief was ordering some one to bring in a light.

Tom Tristram ran out into the hall, and returned with a burning torch; the red light fell upon pillar and vaulted roof, upon the jewelled altar, and upon the motionless form of the dead bride-groom. But the priest, the bride, and the armed men who had just now been gathered about the altar, had all alike disappeared.

"I should think," commented Tom Tristram, "that old Nick had taken them all, but for the fact that the bride has vanished like the others."

Eagerly Peter and Ian MacGregor examined the arched niches by the altar, until at last they came to a way of egress, which led into a narrow stone passage. The passage ended in a small, vaulted chamber, the outer door of which was open, admitting the cold night air and the driving snow.

There were numerous footprints in the snow at the threshold of the chamber, and it was evident that Mary Mac-Gregor had been carried off through this chamber.

"We must follow the trail speedily, before the snow covers it," said Peter. "I will go back and tell Rob Roy of our discovery."

He hastened back into the chapel, which was empty; thence he hurried into the hall of the castle. The Mac-Gregors had thrown lighted torches here and there, in order to fire the building in several places at once, and the hangings on the walls were burning fiercely.

"None shall meddle with the homes of the MacGregors without rueing it," said Rob Roy.

And Peter was ready enough to admit that the destruction of the castle was only an act of justice, and that a woman who had shown so little pity to one of her own sex richly deserved to see her house given to the flames.

But rescue of the kidnapped girl was of more urgent importance than vengeance, and Rob Roy very speedily bade his men desist from plunder, and follow him. Their way was lighted by the flames of the burning castle as they followed the trail of their enemies.

CHAPTER VI.
RESCUED.

The falling snow was fast covering the footmarks of the fugitive Grahames and their allies. They had two or three horses with them, upon which, presumably, Douglas had hoped to travel forward with his bride after the cere-mony; now the horses served to help Douglas's sister and her associates to escape for a time from the vengeance of the Macgregors.

"They have taken Mary and the priest with them," said Peter, who was struggling through the snow, still foremost in the pursuit. "Why should they burden themselves with her, since Douglas is slain?"

"Oh! just to be revenged upon us for his death," replied Ian. "But we shall overtake them before long."

"The trail is failing," said Peter. "I can hardly distinguish the marks now."

Rob Roy pushed to the front, as more used to tracking fugitives, whether human or four-footed, and he led the party on for a time, until he had to confess at a certain point, where two valleys met, that even he was baffled.

The stars were shining through rifts

in the clouds although the snow still continued to fall. There was little enough light by which to search for a trail that it would have been difficult enough to pick up even in broad daylight.

"I have found something," cried Tom Tristram, after the whole party had been beating about for some time, near the place where two ways met. "I have found the track they went."

Peter hastened to him, and discovered him holding a small round object in the palm of his hand.

"Why, you rascal," said Peter, angrily, "I thought you had found footprints. How can a stone help us?"

"'Tis no stone, sir," said Peter, "but a bead. I think the holy man dropped a bead from his rosary, which shows that he was carried this way," and he pointed up one of the valleys.

Search was made further along this way, and another bead was found.

"It seems to me," said Peter, "that we have a friend in the priest. He knew we should pursue the Grahames, and he knew that the snow would fill their footprints, so he dropped the beads of his rosary to guide us."

It was as Peter supposed; the pursuers were guided for several yards by beads, until there could be no doubt as to which way the fugitives had travelled.

"The good man has shed his rosary," said Tom, when they had picked up the last bead. "Heaven help us if we lose their trail again."

The valley path ascended, until at length a place was reached whence several tracks seemed to radiate.

"We shall never overtake them now," groaned Peter. "Which way have they gone? We are surely lost amongst these frightful mountains."

"Nay, sir," said Tom, "I don't think we shall lose ourselves so long as we have the chief with us; and we have not lost the enemy either," he added, eagerly. "Look here!" And again he picked up something from the ground.

"What is it?" asked Peter.

"A crumpled sheet of paper, sir."

"'Tis a leaf from a breviary," said Peter, examining it.

The MacGregors were called together by Ian and, once more put upon the right track by the priest, hastened fiercely after their enemies.

At frequent intervals they came upon crumpled leaves of the priest's breviary, and were thus assured that they were following in the right direction.

Towards daybreak the snow ceased, and just as the pursuers came to the last page of the priest's book the marks of hoofs became discernible again.

Although they had been travelling so long, the Highlanders seemed quite unwearied, and upon the sight of footprints they hastened on with fresh eagerness. When the red sun rose they saw beneath them the placid waters of Loch Lomond, and hastening along the high table-land in front of them, they beheld the prey they had followed all night.

With a fierce cry the MacGregors drew their claymores and broke into a run. The weary Grahames and their friends, who had Mary in their midst, hurried on and took up a position on the top of a snow-covered knoll.

This was speedily surrounded by the MacGregors, who were all shouting their war-cry.

"Spare the priest and the woman," cried Rob Roy, as his clansmen began swarming up the knoll or hillock upon which their enemies stood, grouped about the two horses that had carried the woman and the priest. As they reached the summit of the hillock each man singled out his opponent, and struck as hard and as skilfully as he could. Even while he was attacking a shock headed clansman Peter saw Mary MacGregor, and rejoiced to know that she was safe. She was on horseback, in front of a grey retainer of the Douglas family, who held her on the crupper of his saddle, and who was striving to push through the clansmen and escape from the combat.

Peter hastily cut down his opponent and dashed forward to release Mary. But her custodian succeeded in breaking through the combatants and was riding off down-hill. Rob Roy himself now ran after the horse, closely followed by Peter and Ian. They followed for some distance, until Mary managed to break loose from the hold of her captor. She fell, with a faint scream, upon the snow, while the horseman rode on and escaped.

In another minute she was in her father's arms.

"We are followed. Hasten, Ian,

xclaimed Rob Roy, glancing behind im. The MacGregors had dispersed n chase of some of the fugitives, but resolute party of the enemy had kept ogether, and were bent upon avenging he death of Jamie Douglas by killing Rob Roy.

Five men, accordingly, were swiftly pproaching the spot where Ian was olding his daughter in his arms. The oor girl was terribly exhausted, although verjoyed at her rescue.

"Hurry down to the shores of the och," said Rob Roy, hastily to Ian. Garoch, you must accompany him to elp the lassie through the snow."

"And you, Rob Roy?" said Peter.

"I will keep off these wolves," and he vaved his claymore in the direction of he five swordsmen who were closing upon hem, and once more sternly bade Peter ee to the escape of Mary.

Peter obeyed forthwith, and helped Ian to support her down the hill-ide, while Rob Roy, with a dirk in one hand and his claymore in the other hand, awaited the onset of the furious oes.

The first man hurled himself upon the hief with the fury of a tiger. But Rob Roy's great length of arm stood him in good stead. The man's sword failed to reach Rob Roy's body, while the chief's claymore at the same moment left his skull. And now two men approached Rob Roy together. They had been a little daunted by their comrade's fall, and there was a moment of irresolution before they attacked the chief.

Rob Roy took advantage of this moment of irresolution. With his left hand he plunged his dirk into one man's shoulder, while he kept off the other with his claymore. Then with the latter he drove the second man backwards until the fellow turned and ran for his life. There were still two men to be accounted for, but these, although they dogged Rob Roy's footsteps for a time, did not attempt to close with him; and he made his way triumphantly after Ian and Peter, who had by now helped Mary down to the water's edge.

"We must hide somewhere in shelter," said Peter, seeing how spent and weary Mary was. He was also conscious of the fact that he himself was at last worn out by twenty-four hours of almost incessant exertion.

"We shall be snug enough in my lair," said Rob Roy; "it is not fifty yards from this spot."

Peter looked about him, but there was no house, not so much as a barn, within sight. However, Rob Roy led his friends by a precipitous path to a fissure in the face of the cliff, and having passed through this they found themselves in a deep cave, which was one of the outlawed chief's favourite hiding places.

He had a store of food and drink hidden away here, dry litter to lie on, arms, powder, candles, and a tinder-box.

And so, although the snow was deep outside and fierce enemies ranged the hills, the chief and his friends rested comfortably enough in the cavern by the lake. At first the occupants of the cavern were too tired to do anything but sleep; so, when a fire had been kindled and a portion of the cave had been curtained off for Mary by the Highlander's plaids, the whole party slept till the evening.

And then they gathered about the fire and supped, and drank, and talked merrily enough.

Mary was prevailed upon to give some account of her recent adventures.

It appeared that James Douglas, who had long been an admirer of Mary's, had been invited by his sister to carry her off. He had first acquired a new estate, and had thought that if he married a MacGregor he would, after their first outburst of just indignation, be safe from the depredations of the MacGregors. But his plans had all gone wrong by reason of the fact that Mary was an unwilling bride, and also because he had foolishly allied himself with Rob Roy's bitterest enemies, the Grahames.

"And where does Jamie Douglas's new land lie?" asked Rob Roy.

"I have forgotten the name of it," said Mary. "I was too distressed and frightened to heed what went on all about me, until I came to my senses in the chapel, and was told that I was Douglas's wife. I asked the priest if that were true, and he said that it was so, but the fault was not his; and, indeed, there was a dirk held on each side of his throat as he spoke to me. And then came the clatter of swords, and I knew the clan had saved me."

"So as to give ye, I hope, to a better husband," said Rob Roy; and then, after motioning to Ian, he withdrew to the mouth of the cave. Ian followed him, and Peter was left alone with Mary.

"Mary," said he, "I am, as you know, an Englishman, and care little for the unsettled way of life that pleases your clansmen. Only for two reasons have I stayed in the Highlands so long. I wish to regain by force or by law, I care not which, my house of Garoch; and I wish, a thousand times more, to win you for my bride. May I hope to do that?"

Mary's answer, when she gave it, was propitious, and so, in that rude concern, Mr. Peter Lambe and the Highland girl plighted their troth.

CHAPTER VII.
AN INTERRUPTED BANQUET.

In the course of a few days Rob Roy and his friends returned to Inversnaid, where Tom Tristram was very glad to see his master again.

"Although," he said, "I knew you would come to no harm so long as you were in company with that old fox, Rob Roy."

This was not a very respectful way of speaking of a Highland chief; but Tom could not be brought to realise that the bare-legged MacGregor was anything very different from the highwayman who at that date infested the English roads.

"And I hope, sir," said Tom, "that we are shortly returning to your honour's own house at Garoch, not that I have any love for the place, but just for the look of the thing, and to show that we are not going to be turned out at the pleasure of anybody."

"We were turned out," said Peter, "by the law of Scotland, but we will show, I hope, that Englishmen can hold their own by the sword, if we once get reinstated in the house."

"Then you will not hold the house by law?" asked Tom.

"No, the law will never be my friend until the rightful king comes back again," said Peter. "But with the aid of Rob Roy we will regain the house, and then hold it by force."

"Then we shall live in a state of siege?" said Tom, rubbing his hands with glee. "I think I can promise the Campbells—if such thieves come nigh us again—many pleasant surprises."

But Peter did not look forward with

any satisfaction to the mode of li[fe] which his servant predicted for hi[m] He wished to marry and settle down i[n] peace, and he had some thoughts o[f] handing the house of Garoch over t[o] Ian MacGregor or to Rob Roy, if [it] should ever be retaken.

The day after their return to the fo[rt] of Inversnaid Rob Roy began to discu[ss] plans for the recapture of Peter['s] house, but while he was thus engage[d] a messenger came to the fort with th[e] news that the priest who had, by h[is] ready wit, enabled the MacGregors t[o] follow and rescue Mary, was a prison[er] in the hands of Duncan Grahame.

When Mary was rescued the Mac[c] Gregors had scattered her captors, a[s] we have seen; but a small body of the[m] rode away, so Tom Tristram was able t[o] affirm, with the priest in their midst.

"Why should they wish to keep th[e] priest with them?" asked Peter, aft[er] hearing the messenger's news.

"Because they forced him into a[n] illegal act," said Rob Roy, "and a[t] Edinburgh he might be a dangerou[s] enemy to them; for if he gave eviden[ce] in the law-courts against them the[re] would be work for the hangman. A[y,] Mr. Lambe, but we will go and delive[r] this priest from his dungeon, and the[n] leave the law to deal with Dunca[n] Grahame and the rest of Jamie Douglas['s] friends."

So the journey to Garoch was post[poned again, and half-a-score me[n] besides Rob Roy and Peter, girded on the[ir] swords to rescue the priest who had she[d] the beads of his rosary in their service.

It appeared that he was imprison[ed] in the turret of a castle belonging t[o] Duncan Grahame. The castle was a[n] isolated building standing in a wil[d] glen on the outskirts of Montrose['s] country. By his late exploit Dunca[n] Grahame had certainly brought hims[elf] within reach of the law; but the law wa[s] just then, slow to act against anyon[e] who enjoyed the protection of the grea[t] Duke of Montrose. However, if th[e] priest got loose, and gave an accoun[t] of his wrongs, in Edinburgh, not eve[n] Montrose's name could shelter Dunca[n] Grahame and the others who had helpe[d] to carry off Mary MacGregor. So Ro[b] Roy resolved that the priest should b[e] let loose, partly out of gratitude t[o] him, and partly in order to be revenge[d] upon the Grahames.

long march brought the rescue
ty within sight of the black castle
re the priest was imprisoned. The
ding stood on the summit of a rocky
overlooking a small lake and at the
d of a glen.

t was evening when the Highlanders
ed within sight of the castle. The
und was now clear of snow, for it was
y spring, and the castle, and the rock
n which it was built, stood out
k against the moonlit waters of the

light shone in one of the turret
dows.

I know this Duncan Grahame," said
Roy, "and if we assault the castle
will kill his prisoner upon the first
m, and afterwards accuse us of his
der."

Then we have come upon a useless
nd," said Peter, "for the priest is
med."

Not so," said Rob Roy, scanning
tower of the castle. "I will out-
this impious wretch who makes war
n women and priests. Well, Gregor,
t have ye seen?" he asked of a
ng man, whom he had sent forward
py upon the castle at close quarters.
he spy replied in Gaelic that there
a feast in progress in the castle.

I heard the sound of pipes," he
, "so I stole round the castle, and
windows on the other side are
laze of light."

That is well," said Rob Roy.
here is a feast taking place, but no
e is laid at table for the priest, and
t, too, is well."

Rob Roy then took from one of his men
oil of strong, fine rope, a hammer,
a bag of long nails.

Come with me, Garoch," he then
to Peter, and after giving some
ructions to his men the chief ad-
ced towards the castle.

He and Peter climbed the rocky hillock
he base of the turret, and Rob Roy,
r listening for a minute, drove two
s firmly into the mortar of the
l, each about breast-high from the
und and a foot apart from one
ther. Then, unbuckling his sword-
t and handing it and his claymore
Peter, the chief mounted to this foot-
d, clinging flat against the face of the
lding, and drove in more nails. The
e was coiled about his waist.

And so, while Peter looked anxiously

on, Rob Roy steadily climbed up the
tower towards the window where the
light was burning. It was a perilous
feat, but he reached the window at last
and looked in and saw the priest, who
was an Irishman, named O'Neill, writing
at a bare table.

"You sent a message to me," said
Rob Roy, calmly, "and I have come."

Father O'Neill looked up and crossed
himself. Then he recognised the Mac-
Gregor tartan, and knew that the man at
the window was no spectral visitor, but
someone who had come to help him out
of his prison.

"You must help me into your prison
before I can get you out of it, Father,"
said Rob Roy.

"Faith, and I'll do that very gladly,"
said the priest, "though I would not do
so if I did not know that no prison is
strong enough to hold Rob Roy for long.
Whisht! If they hear me it'll be all up
with poor Father O'Neill."

The priest, who was a strong, muscular
man, wrenched away an iron bar that
crossed the window, and that had kept
Rob Roy from entering, and then gave
a hand to the chief, whom he pulled into
his own room.

At the same moment they heard a
terrific uproar below. The MacGregors,
by a preconcerted arrangement with
Rob Roy, had made an attack upon the
castle on the side facing the lake, where
the principal door was.

"'Tis my lads tapping at the castle
door," said Rob Roy, with a smile.
"Now, father, we may not need the
rope, but just by way of precaution
do you fasten it firmly and throw one
end out of the window. It will reach
to the ground."

Father O'Neill obeyed orders with
alacrity; the thought of liberty was
delightful to him after some weeks of
dreary imprisonment.

"The rope touches the ground, but
there is a man waiting below," he said.

"That is Mr. Lambe, a friend of mine,"
replied Rob Roy, who was standing by
the door of the room with his dirk in his
hand.

"What are you going to do, Mac-
Gregor?" asked the priest, seeing the
dirk.

"That depends upon who it is that
opens this door, Father O'Neill." Then,
as the uproar below grew louder, he
added, "I think you had better go

down by the rope, Father; it is knotted, and there are footholds to aid your descent."

"I hope there will be no bloodshed on my account," said the priest.

Rob Roy would give no guarantee of that, but quietly helped the priest to climb out of the window. When he saw that he was safely started on his journey to the ground Rob Roy stood again by the door, with his dirk ready.

He soon heard hasty footsteps on the stairs outside, and then voices.

"Do your business quickly," said someone.

"'Tis ill work," replied another voice.

"Then the sooner it is despatched the better."

"But is it needful?"

"Needful, you fool! If the MacGregors got hold of him we shall be outlawed at least. Eh! you poor trembling body. I will do the deed myself."

The next moment the door was unlocked, and in stepped Duncan Grahame, a huge sandy-haired man, whose ferocious face was now flushed by drinking. He held a claymore in his hand, and his object was to kill the defenceless priest whose word might bring him to the gallows, and whom he expected to find in the turret room.

He gazed stupidly round the room. Rob Roy shut the door behind him, and then leapt forward and caught Grahame by the throat with his left hand, while with the right hand he held the dirk to his heart.

"Drop your claymore, Duncan, or you're a dead man," he hissed.

The choking Duncan at last obeyed; Rob Roy flung him back against the wall with contempt, and then stooped and picked up his sword.

"Ay! you would kill an unarmed man, would you, Duncan?" he said, "I will not do that. I will leave the lawyers and hangmen to do that to you, Duncan Grahame, and it's not Montrose himself who will be able to save you when Father O'Neill tells his story in Edinburgh."

Grahame, with a hand upon his aching throat, was gazing in terror at Rob Roy, quite unable, in his surprise and confusion, to account for the presence of the outlawed chief and the absence of Father O'Neill.

Rob Roy left him staring, went out of the room, and locked the door securely.

"Have you done it?" whisp[e] someone on the dark stairway.

Rob Roy gave the questioner a ran[d] kick that sent him toppling to the [foot] of the stairs, stunned and senseless.

Then the chief descended boldly [to] the hall of the castle into which [his] men had just forced their way, in spi[te] superior numbers.

A wild fight was going on; claym[ores] were crashing upon bucklers, as mem[bers] of the rival clans of MacGregor [and] Grahame fought in all corners of [the] hall at once. Two men were slas[hing] at one another upon the banquet t[able] their feet amidst the dishes and w[ine] flagons. A terrified servant was hi[ding] under the table. Dogs were bark[ing] or plundering the neglected dishes, [and] altogether there was a good dea[l of] noise, if there was little serious bloods[hed].

Into this scene of confusion sta[lked] Rob Roy, armed with Duncan Graha[me's] claymore. Suddenly he raised the slo[gan] of his clan; the Grahames beheld [him] in their midst and were startled ou[t of] their fortitude. They scattered a[bout] the hall, and the MacGregors, who [had] been waging an unequal fight aga[inst] superior numbers, rallied together, [and] marched triumphantly out of the d[oor.] They had disturbed the Grahame[s in] their own banquetting hall, and [had] rescued Father O'Neill.

Beyond this Rob Roy did not wis[h to] go, for he never shed blood needlessl[y].

Keeping together in a solid, unassail[able] band, the MacGregors left the ca[stle] and bitter were the scoffs they f[lung] back at the Grahames as they wen[t].

Peter and Father O'Neill were wai[ting] at the rear of the castle, and the w[hole] company now set out upon the re[turn] journey to Inversnaid. But, so [as] not to return empty-handed, they [first] of all collected together as many [of] Duncan Grahame's cattle as they c[ould] find, and drove them before them.

CHAPTER VIII.
A NARROW ESCAPE.

A few days after the rescue of [the] priest, Peter set out early in the mor[ning] intending to visit Mary at her fat[her's] house. Rob Roy, who wished to [visit] some relatives who dwelt not far [from] Ian MacGregor's house, accompa[nied] him, the pair going on foot across [the] lonely hills.

At noon they halted at an inn which stood beside the mountain road, and made a frugal meal.

Then Rob Roy departed upon business of his own, having promised to meet Peter again at nightfall, at a given tryst-ing-place, so that they might bear one another company back to Inversnaid.

This being arranged, Peter made his way to the house of Ian MacGregor, where he spent the day.

The moon was up when he left the house, and he walked speedily over the heather to the trysting-place, where Rob Roy was awaiting him.

It was getting late when they drew near to a small village, and Rob Roy, seeing that the English laird was growing tired, proposed that they should pass the night in the village inn, and resume their journey in the morning.

"I am very willing to do that," said Peter, "if you can safely tarry here."

"My clan can protect me," said Rob Roy. "I shall be in no danger here, I assure you."

So they entered a comfortable inn in the middle of the village.

A man was sitting by the fire of the room into which they were ushered, and, after talking with them for a little while, he rose, and remarked that it was time he was going home.

"My good wife will have somewhat to say to me," he said with a sheepish smile, "if I tarry over long, or take home an extra dram with me."

Rob Roy laughed. "Eh!" he said, "trust the lassies for keeping a man in order when once he is married. You mind that, Mr. Lambe. Yet you shall stay and have another dram, good man, and if your wife flouts you tell her you were compelled to drink by Rob Roy."

The man complied with Rob Roy's good-humoured order, and then went out.

For a time Peter and the chief re-mained by the fire, and were about to retire to bed when there was a knock-ing at the door, and the man who had tarried to take an extra dram returned again.

"What!" laughed Rob Roy, "has your wife sent you out with a flea in your lug, or has she shut the door in your face, good man?"

"No," said the man, with a look of grave concern on his face, "but as I was going home I was put in mind of the trouble that has come upon Mrs. Campbell, who lives in the cottage by the bridge, for I could hear her wailing. She was a MacGregor before she married, and I thought 'perhaps Rob Roy can help her, as he is here, so I came back to tell you of it."

"What is her trouble?" asked Rob Roy, ever ready to be of help to those in distress, especially if they were of his own clan.

"Her husband is dying, and to-morrow the miller's going to take away her cow for a debt which she says is not a just debt. I know not how that may be, but the miller's a hard man, and the law ever favours those with the most money."

Rob Roy's face hardened. "The miller may haply find himself in his own mill-dam," he said. "I will see to this." For he knew that the loss of a cow was a serious matter to a Scotch peasant. "I will go at once," he added, "and tell this poor woman that I will either pay her debt or drown the miller, according as his claim is a good one or a bad one."

Saying this the chief rose, and Peter with him.

The Englishman did not like the hang-dog look of the messenger who had thus summoned Rob Roy away from the fire-side, so he buckled on his sword, which he had put aside.

When they were outside the inn the messenger pointed out to them the house where, he said, the distressed peasant woman lived, and then, pro-fessing to be in fear of consequences if he stayed any longer away from home, went off in an opposite direction.

Peter and the chief walked down the moonlit street and across the bridge, and Rob Roy entered the small garden of the house and knocked at the door.

A surly man put his head out of the window.

"Who's there?" he asked.

"I've come to give a message to Mary Campbell," said Rob Roy.

"There's no Mary Campbell here, so get away with you, or I'll souse you with cold water," replied the occupant of the cottage, who was not best pleased at having his slumbers broken, and he slammed the window.

"I mistrusted that hang-dog fellow," said Peter. "We have been tricked."

" But to what purpose ? " said the chief, whose face wore an angry look as they re-crossed the bridge.

His question was quickly answered. No sooner were they in the middle of the bridge than three men with drawn swords came upon it from the end next the village.

" There are two of them," one of these men exclaimed.

Presumably they had expected to catch Rob Roy alone.

" That rascal at the inn has set these men on to me," said Rob Roy.

" And sent you hither on a fool's errand so that they might catch you outside the village where none will hear and come to your help," said Peter. " However —— " and he drew his sword from its sheath.

The three men were running forward, having apparently made up their minds to attack the chief. And, indeed, from a pecuniary point of view it was at that time well worth anybody's while to attempt to catch the outlaw, in consequence of the price that was set upon his head. But the moonlight soon revealed to Rob Roy the fact that these were no chance seekers after blood money, for the midmost man of the three was Duncan Grahame, who had played so prominent a part in carrying off Mary MacGregor, and who was himself in danger of outlawry for his share in that night's work.

The man at the inn, knowing of the Grahame's hostility to Rob Roy, had informed them that the chief was in the village and, as Peter had guessed, had inveigled Rob Roy on to the bridge, where there were no houses to afford him refuge and where he was hemmed in by his foes ; for, upon turning, Peter saw that two other swordsmen had followed them on to the bridge.

" Three in front and two behind," said Rob Roy, sharply. " Follow me, Garoch."

And instantly he turned and ran at the two who had sprung from some ambush to cut off their retreat from the bridge.

These two heroes seeing the furious chief coming towards them, with his claymore glistening in the moonshine, and his face aflame with rage, turned and ran for their lives.

Then, turning again, Rob Roy called to Peter to follow him, and, over the central arch of the bridge they encountered Duncan Grahame and his two supporters. Peter singled out one of these and cut the man's fingers so badly at the first blow that the fellow threw down his sword and ran away. Duncan Grahame's second supporter had already felt the edge of Rob Roy's claymore ; Peter brought him down too badly wounded to continue the fight, with a cut at his head, and then only Duncan Grahame was left.

He was a tall, powerful man, and he had with him his targe or shield, as well as his claymore, whereas Rob Roy was unprovided with that defence.

" Leave him to me," said Rob Roy to Peter, and the latter, who was breathless with fighting, respected the enraged chief's wish and stood against the parapet of the bridge, while the two stalwart Highlanders hammered sparks from one another's swords as they fought in the cold moonlight.

" If Rob Roy falls I shall avenge him,' Peter told himself.

Thwack ! The MacGregor's sword came down on the Grahame's uplifted target, and then he leapt back to avoid a cruel blow. Again he slashed a Grahame's head ; again the shield caught the furious blow.

Then the two swords clashed together sparks flew again, and both men began to grow breathless.

They drew apart for a few seconds both flushed with rage.

" Eh, you cur," said Rob Roy, " you thought to catch me asleep, with your treacherous tales of poor peasant women. You priest-murderer, 'tis not the likes of you should meddle with armed men."

Again they closed, and Rob Roy's blows were rained so hard at Grahame who could not get within striking distance of the nimble and long-armed MacGregor, that he had to use claymore and target to defend himself, and at last the former was struck from his numbed hand.

He cowered down, his shield held up to protect his head from the blow he expected to follow. But Rob Roy dropped his own sword, stepped forward grasped his opponent round the middle and, after a struggle, threw him heavily over the parapet of the bridge into the brawling river below.

Then he picked up his sword, and Grahame's sword, the latter as a trophy of the fight.

"I might have killed him, Garoch," he said, "but I would not rob the gallows of its due, and Father O'Neill has laid information against the man. He will scramble out of the water by-and-by, I daresay, and indeed I hope he will, for it would not be fitting that so poor a cur should die at the hands of a chief."

And the justly indignant chief of Clan Gregor stalked off the bridge in company with his friend.

After this instance of the dangers of travel, Peter besought Rob Roy to return at once to the fort of Inversnaid; and so, after an arduous march, they reached their harbour of refuge by daybreak.

CHAPTER IX.

The English Laird Enjoys His Own Again.

And now Rob Roy declared that he was prepared to reinstate Peter in his house.

"But," he said, "it is cold comfort to go to your house without a wife by your side, Mr. Lambe. And since you and my kinsman's daughter are both of the Roman Church, why should not Father O'Neill marry you before you return to Garoch?"

"You forget, Rob Roy," replied Peter, "that my house must be regained by blows, and perhaps held by the sword, until King James comes to his own again."

"I do not think so," replied Rob Roy; and both he and Father O'Neill, who chanced to be present, laughed heartily; whereat Peter was much mystified.

"The house is, I hear, at present occupied by some officer of the law," continued Peter.

"Ay, it is that," said Rob Roy.

"He will have some sturdy rogues who will contest my right to enter, and he will have the law of Scotland on his side to turn me out again if I do retake possession of the place. I cannot take a wife into a house that may be the scene of constant brawls."

"Do you marry your wife, Mr. Lambe, and leave it to me and Father O'Neill to see that you are allowed to settle peaceably at Garoch," replied Rob Roy.

So Peter, nothing loth, rode over to Mary's house, to fix the date of the wedding. This event, they soon decided, should take place in a few weeks' time.

In the meanwhile Rob Roy left the fort of Inversnaid in possession of some of his clansmen, and roamed from one place of retreat to another. Peter met him at an inn at Tyndrum, and represented to him that he would like to take possession of his house and get it in order for his bride before the wedding; but Rob Roy declared this to be impossible.

"You shall first of all marry your wife," he said, "and then I will go to Garoch with you, with fifty armed men at my back if you wish it; but no fighting will be needed."

"But how about this Campbell, the knight who turned me out of the house?"

"Oh, the matter has passed out of his hands. He will not resist you, and I hope, after to-night, he will inform against no more Jacobites."

"And why so?" asked Peter.

"I expect him here," said Rob Roy.

"He will be a venturesome man to visit you. Do you mean to say the rascal is coming here?"

"I sent three of my men to invite him hither," said Rob Roy.

"Oh, that explains matters," said Peter. "An invitation of that sort cannot easily be refused."

The shades of evening fell, and Peter remained in company with Rob Roy and others of the MacGregor clan. At last, when all were merry over their whisky, the door of the room was opened, and the offending knight of the Campbell clan, much disordered as to his attire and flushed as to his countenance, was thrust into the room.

He was greeted with a cheer of derision, and was then held before Rob Roy, who was to be his judge. His chief offence seemed to be that he had evicted a MacGregor, by legal process, from some land at Glendochart. Alarmed by the hostile faces all about him, Campbell readily consented to sign a paper the effect of which was to reinstate the evicted MacGregor.

"And now, my good friends, let me go," he said.

Peter in vain strove to make his voice heard above the chatter of the clansmen. He would have had Campbell sign a paper reinstating him also; but his petition did not reach the ears of Rob Roy, who was giving some orders relative to the captive.

In a few minutes, with bursts of noisy laughter, the clansmen were hurrying their prisoner through the darkness to some unknown destination, and Peter followed out of curiosity. He remembered how Rob Roy had said that Campbell would inform against no more Jacobites.

"I hope they are not going to hang the poor wretch," he said to himself; "he is a poor, pitiful rogue, but it is sorry work to hang a helpless man."

It looked at last rather as though the wild clansmen intended to drown the luckless knight, for they halted at the edge of a large pool.

Now this pool, though at that time Peter knew it not, was no ordinary pool. It had been blessed by St. Fillan, whose name it bore, and was supposed to possess special virtues.

His gay clothing was torn from him, and, with a rope about his middle, he was cast into the holy waters.

The victim spluttered, and swore, and protested; but he had meddled with a MacGregor, and the MacGregors were not disposed to let him off lightly.

It was a few days after this affair that the wedding of the English laird took place, amidst great festivities, and the day after the wedding Peter and his wife were escorted back to Garoch by Rob Roy, Father O'Neill, and a few of Rob Roy's followers.

Peter was still at a loss to understand how they were to take peaceable possession of the house, and Rob Roy and the priest still continued to treat his doubts as a great joke.

When the party arrived at the house Rob Roy himself knocked at the door, which was opened by some understrapper of the law.

"Here is Mr. Lambe, come back to his own house again," said the chief.

The understrapper looked alarmed at the sight of the MacGregor plaid, and went to confer with someone of greater importance. In the meantime Peter led his bride into the house, and the clansmen gathered about him.

Suddenly a door opened, and Campbell, the man who had so recently suffered such indignities at the hands of the MacGregors, entered the hall, for he chanced to be in the house.

"What does this mean?" he stammered, "I signed no paper reinstating Mr. Lambe. This is an illegal trespass."

"St. Fillan has not cured ye yet of covetousness, then?" said Rob Roy.

The knight began to grow frightened again.

"I covet no man's goods. This house was granted to another, at my instigation, but he is dead, and I am holding it till his heir comes to take possession," he said.

"Then you may go back to your own country, Campbell," said Rob Roy, "for the heir has come."

"What mean you?"

"I mean, that by your help, the law has secured Mr. Lambe in possession of this house. You took care to see that James Douglas's title to it was a good one."

"Ay, it was granted to James Douglas; but he is dead, and it passes to his next-of-kin."

"That is to say, to his widow. Here she is, but she is now Mr. Lambe's wife, and what is hers is her husband's. And so, man Campbell, you've wrought a crooked course to your own confusion, and the English laird can laugh at you."

And Peter did laugh, much surprised at the turn affairs had taken. Father O'Neill was able to prove that Mary had actually, in the eyes of the law, been Douglas's wife for a few minutes before his death, so Campbell had nothing more to say, but presently retired, discomfited, amidst the jeers of the MacGregors.

"And so," said Tom Tristram, "we have triumphed over all thieves and traitors with the help of Rob Roy, and are come safely home again."

And the English laird remained in possession of his house and of Rob Roy's friendship as long as he dwelt in the Highlands of Scotland.

THE END.